Danny, Who Fell in a Hole

Danny, Who Fell in a Hole

CARY FAGAN

Illustrations by Milan Pavlovic

GROUNDWOOD BOOKS
HOUSE OF ANANSI PRESS
TORONTO / BERKELEY

Groundwood Books/House of Anansi Press
110 Spadina Avenue, Suite 801
Toronto, Ontario M5V 2K4
or c/o Publishers Group West
1700 Fourth Street, Berkeley, CA 94710

We acknowledge for their financial support of our publishing program the
Canada Council for the Arts, the Government of Canada through the Canada
Book Fund (CBF) and the Ontario Arts Council.
Library and Archives Canada Cataloguing in Publication

 Canada Council **Conseil des Arts**
for the Arts **du Canada**

 ONTARIO ARTS COUNCIL
CONSEIL DES ARTS DE L'ONTARIO

Fagan, Cary
Danny, who fell in a hole / written by Cary Fagan ; illustrated
by Milan Pavlovic.
Issued also in an electronic format.
ISBN 978-1-55498-311-7 (bound).—ISBN 978-1-55498-312-4 (pbk.)
I. Pavlovic, Milan II. Title.
PS8561.A375D36 2013   jC813'.54   C2012-905159-4

Cover illustration by Milan Pavlovic
Design by Michael Solomon

Groundwood Books is committed to protecting our natural environment. As
part of our efforts, the interior of this book is printed on paper that contains
100% post-consumer recycled fibers, is acid-free and is processed chlorine-free.

Printed and bound in Canada

 MIX
Paper from
responsible sources
FSC® C004071
www.fsc.org

 ANCIENT FOREST ™
FRIENDLY

For Paul Lowry —
childhood friend, rival, inspiration

1

Big News

"IT'S REALLY NOTHING to worry about," Danny's mother said.

"Think of it as an adventure," Danny's father said. "That's what life really is, right? Full of surprises."

Danny and his older brother, Doug, sat in the two matching armchairs in the living room. All around them were cardboard boxes. The boxes were full of their stuff: books, framed pictures, shoes and baseball mitts.

The boxes hadn't been there that morning.

Doug was slumped in his chair plucking his ukulele. But Danny was sitting bolt upright.

His hands were holding onto the armrests as if the chair might start to buck like a wild horse.

His parents were sitting on the sofa holding hands and looking at Danny and his brother with the exact same faces. Danny knew those expressions well. Usually they meant that his parents had volunteered them all to paint an outdoor mural, or perform in an amateur theater festival, or "engage" in some other artistic "happening."

But nothing had prepared him for this.

Doug began to strum his ukulele and mumble some lyrics he was working on. His brother was almost finished high school and was already taking driving lessons. He and Danny used to be best buddies. They used to go to movies and build forts. Doug even used to call him Dannio.

Then his brother didn't want to hang around together anymore. He stayed in his room listening to weird music and drawing pictures. All his pictures were of cars crashing, or buses crashing, or trains or planes or spaceships crashing. There was always lots of flames and blood.

Danny's parents said the pictures were "brilliant, expressive and honest," and they stuck them up on the walls.

When he wasn't drawing, Doug was making up songs on his ukulele. They were mostly about cars and planes crashing, too, and how even while crashing he could only think about some girl or other. When Doug's friends came over, they did pointless stuff like stare at the covers of old vinyl record albums. Or they would lie on their backs on the floor and look up at the ceiling.

Danny remembered all this now because he wondered what Doug was thinking.

What his parents had just said made absolutely no sense. They might as well have been talking in Serbian or some other language he didn't have a clue about.

"So let me get this straight," Doug said, pulling a stick of gum from his pocket and folding it into his mouth. "You're getting a divorce."

"No, no, absolutely not," Danny's father said quickly. "That's not it at all. We are not getting a divorce. We're not even separating. Your mom and I love each other. Did you hear me? We're just going to live apart. For a year. Or maybe two."

"You know how much we've always valued our creativity," Danny's mother said. "Your father and I have dreams. Artistic dreams. We want to pursue them before it's too late. Before we're too old. Those dreams are taking us to different places for a while. You understand the need to fulfill yourself. After all, you both have dreams, too. Doug, you want to be a songwriter."

Doug rolled his eyes.

"And, Danny, you want to be an actuary."

"I never said that. My teacher did, because I'm good at math. I don't even know what an actuary is."

"The point is," his father said, "we want to be good role models for our two great sons. We want you to know that you can be whatever you want. And the best way to show that is to do it ourselves. Right, Sheila?"

"That's right."

"Tell us again what you're going to do," said Doug, snapping his gum.

"Your father wants to be an opera singer in New York City."

"And your mother wants to move to Banff, Alberta, and bake cheesecakes."

"I don't even know where Banff is," Danny complained, his voice rising.

"It's out west, in the Rocky Mountains," his mother said. "It's one of the most beautiful places in the world. You can see bears! You can slide on a glacier."

"So we get to live in New York and also in Banff?" Doug said. "I guess that's cool."

"That's right," said Danny's father. "You're going to live with Mom during the school year. And you'll spend the summer and holidays with me. In Banff you can go skiing every day."

"I don't know how to ski," Danny said.

"It's a great opportunity to learn. And New York has theater and music and anything else you could want. You are two very lucky boys. Your friends are going to envy you. Won't they, Sheila?"

"I'll say. We figured that you would understand, Doug. You're the creative one, like your dad and me. Danny, we knew it would be a little harder for you. You're the level-headed one in the family. It's not your fault that you're not creative like the rest of us."

"But you have my painting up on the fridge," Danny said. "The sunset that I did at school."

"Sunsets are cliché," Doug muttered, strumming his ukulele again.

"To a common-sense person like you," his mother went on, "this might seem very impractical. But dreams are not practical, Dan-

ny. Vincent van Gogh wasn't practical. Bob Dylan wasn't practical."

His parents leaned forward, as if that would help him understand.

Danny said nothing. He was trying to take in what he had heard. He and Doug wouldn't live with both his parents at the same time? They were going to move away to Banff? And also New York?

Danny looked around the room again. For the first time he understood why all the moving boxes were there.

"What about our house?" he said. "What about my room?"

"The house is going up for sale tomorrow," his father said. "We've got your room packed up already. But you'll have a new room. You'll have two new rooms."

"But I like my room. I don't want to live in two places. And what about Thwack?"

Thwack was their dog. Danny had named

him when he was little because Thwack would get so excited that he would run straight into a wall. *Thwack!*

"Come to think of it," he said. "Where is Thwack?"

Danny's mother looked at Danny's father.

"He's at his wonderful new home. On a farm."

Danny stood up. "You gave away my dog?"

"Now, he wasn't just your dog," his father said.

"At least I don't have to walk him anymore," Doug sniffed.

"How can you say that?" Danny cried. "Thwack was part of our family!" He turned to his parents. "Would you give me away?"

"Now you're being a little ridiculous," his father said.

"But it's understandable," his mother smiled. "In Banff we can get a new pet. Something small and easy to take care of. Maybe a hamster."

"I don't want a hamster!" Danny shouted. "I want Thwack. I want my room and my park and my school! I want my two parents sitting at the dinner table, not just one of them! You didn't ask me! You didn't consult with me! Well, thanks very much but I say no."

"What?" said his father.

"No, no, no!"

"Hey, Dannio," said his brother. "It's not that big a deal."

Danny sprang from the chair. He had never felt so angry in his life.

Who did they think they were? What about parental responsibility? What about kids coming first?

He wanted to run around and smash all the lamps in the house. He wanted to throw his mother's cake dishes across the kitchen and toss his father's opera CDs out the window as if they were Frisbees.

But what he did was run.

2

Falling

AND RUN HE DID. Across the room, down the front hall. Then he grabbed his backpack and ran out the front door.

He ran across the lawn, up the sidewalk, around the corner.

Without stopping, he struggled to put on his backpack.

He ran past Essex Street, Winkler Avenue, Nordheim Boulevard.

He ran past Gornick's Pharmacy, the Strong Brew Coffee Shop, Frida's Clothing Exchange and the Blue Skies Credit Union.

When he reached Harlow Street he paused to catch his breath, leaning his hands on his knees. His heart beat fast. His breath came quick and shallow.

What right did they have to wreck his life? Did a kid have to put up with any sort of behavior from his parents?

No, he did not. But what could he do about it?

Danny didn't know. All he knew was that he had a terrible energy inside him. If he didn't let it out, he would explode.

So he started running again.

He ran up Harlow and across the park where some little kids were being pushed on the swings by their parents.

Sure, you're happy now, Danny wanted to cry out. But look out! They're going to turn on you. They're going to go off to "fulfill" themselves!

He passed a plaza of small shops — shoe repair, bagel bakery, discount eyewear. Then a row of low apartment buildings that he didn't recognize. His chest hurt and his legs were starting to ache, but he kept going.

He passed an unfamiliar school and then an office building. Next to the building was a construction site.

NEW DELUXE CONDOMINIUMS! LUXURY LIVING!

There was a fence around the site, but the gate was open and Danny stepped through. He saw some bulldozers and other construction equipment on the chewed-up ground.

No people were around, probably because it was late Friday afternoon.

Danny ran across the site. He had to jump over wooden boards and dodge piles of bricks. He picked up speed, lengthening his stride. He saw a broken pipe in front of him, jumped and felt...

Air?

Instead of landing, Danny began to fall. And he kept falling downward, his arms and legs flailing in the air.

Fear overwhelmed him.

I don't want to die! Danny screamed, although it didn't come out as words. All he could see was the dark earth wall flashing by. He reached out, trying to grab something, but there was nothing to grab.

He felt as if he were falling for a long, long time, although in fact it couldn't have been more than seconds. He thought of his mother and his father and his big brother. He saw their faces looking mournful but resigned, as if they knew they couldn't save him.

They were mouthing words he couldn't hear. It looked as though they were saying "Goodbye, Danny..."

He hit the ground. *Thud*. The soft earth and the backpack broke his fall. But still it hurt, and he yelped.

Dirt flew up into his eyes and mouth. But he didn't brush it away. He just curled up on his side and lay there without moving.

3

Inventory

DANNY WASN'T ASLEEP and he wasn't unconscious, but for a long time he lay curled up on the soft earth. The blow from the impact of landing had left him feeling stunned. Only slowly did he begin to move his fingers, and then his toes. The back of his head, his shoulder and his hip hurt. He moaned a little.

He brushed the earth from his face, sat up and blinked several times.

He was at the bottom of a very deep hole. A hole that must have been dug by one of those enormous digging machines. It was deep and long and almost oval shaped. It was about four times longer than his bedroom at home — or what used to be his home.

The hole ought to have a fence around it, Danny thought. Like a swimming pool. It was dangerous. He bet he could sue the condominium company for a lot of money — maybe even enough to buy a house and live by himself.

Would that be legal, a kid living on his own? Probably not.

Danny looked up. Far above him he could see the opening and the oval of blue sky.

He cupped his hands around his mouth and shouted.

"Hey!"

And then again.

"Hey, hey, HEYYY!"

The sound of his voice was absorbed by the surrounding wall of earth, so that it was no louder than a whisper. Nobody would hear him unless the person was actually looking down into the hole, and maybe not even then.

Danny looked down and saw a stone by his foot. He picked it up and then reached way back, flinging the stone as hard as he could.

The stone went up about five feet before it thumped against the wall and fell down again.

Throwing straight up was a lot harder than it looked.

Danny picked up the stone again, but this time he walked to the middle of the hole. He reached back and waited longer before opening his hand and sending the stone as straight up as he could.

The stone soared up. It was well below the opening of the hole before it seemed to hover a moment. Then it started to fall again.

The stone was falling straight toward Danny.

He put his hands over his head and bent down just in time for the stone to smack against his arm.

"Ow!"

The spot where the stone hit turned red and began to throb. He'd have a bruise for sure. That wasn't too brilliant.

Wait a minute, Danny thought. My cell-phone!

How could he have forgotten? One quick call and he was out of here.

He took off his backpack, brushed off the dirt and found his phone in the side pocket. He was worried that the impact from the fall had broken it. But, no, it was still working.

He was about to hit his home number when he stopped.

Did he really want to phone home? After what they were trying to do to him? After giving away his dog?

No, he did not. Instead, he found his grand-father's number in the directory and pressed the green Talk button. At least his grandfather actually loved and cared about him.

NO SERVICE flashed on the screen.

"Oh, come on!" Danny cried. "Come on, come on, come on!" He shook the phone and tried again, walking all around the bottom of the hole.

Nothing.

Danny put the phone back into his backpack. In a sudden rush of panic he tried to climb the wall. He ran forward and began to claw at the earth with his fingers while he tried to get a foothold with his sneakers.

But the wall was packed hard earth. Too hard for him to push into for a handhold. The bottoms of his shoes slid down without getting any traction.

He saw a root sticking out just above his head. He jumped up and managed to grab it with one hand. With a tremendous effort he held on, his feet dangling a few inches from the ground.

But there wasn't anything higher to grab onto. He had to let go.

Beads of sweat broke out on his forehead. His fingers hurt from grasping the root so tightly.

All right, all right, he told himself. It was time to calm down and take stock of the situation. After all, he might not be creative, but he was smart. Even his no-good parents said so. He could use his brain to figure out what to do.

Number one. Where was he?

At the bottom of a hole.

Number two. Was there a way to get himself out?

Not that he was able to see.

Number three. Was there a way to get help?

Also negative.

Which meant that until somebody found him, he was going to be stuck down here.

His parents would realize he was missing, but probably not for a while. No doubt they would phone the neighbors and some of the parents of other kids at school. It might take them a few hours to find him. Which meant that he was going to be down here for a while.

He couldn't be stupid. He had to take it easy. He had to keep his head on straight.

But even as Danny gave himself this lecture, his heart continued to pound. He needed something to keep him focused and calm. His parents always said he was practical, as if it were some kind of defect.

Well, then, he would be practical.

Here was an idea. He could take an inventory of everything in his backpack.

He flipped back the flap and began to pull things out of it, laying them on the ground.

Three peanut-butter granola bars.

One stainless-steel water thermos, one-third filled with water.

One oversized sweatshirt with a grape-juice stain on it.

Several school textbooks and workbooks.

One cellphone, useless.

One full-sized plastic garbage bag, intended for tomorrow's volunteer park clean-up.

One harmonica.

Four paper clips.

Nail clippers.

One pencil.

One metal ruler.

One DVD of *School for Zombies 3*.

One by one, Danny put each of the objects back into his pack. All except for the harmonica, which his grandfather gave him last weekend. Doug didn't like going to visit the "old geezer" as he called him, but Danny always looked forward to it. His grandfather had a box of amazing old photographs. Some showed him in his army uniform, or leaning against a gleaming car with giant fins on the back. In one photo he was on the beach holding a bathing beauty (who later became Danny's grandmother). Danny's grandfather still had his traveling-salesman's case full of googly-eyed glasses and trick playing cards, kaleidoscopes and whirligigs.

The harmonica had been in there, too. Danny thought it would be cool to be a great blues harmonica player, so he was glad to have it.

He slid down against the dirt wall until he was sitting. Then he put the harmonica to his mouth and blew. It would have been nice if some heartbreaking blues came out — music that matched the mood Danny was in.

But instead, all that came out was a wheezy note, like the sound of a donkey with a cold.

4

Blah!

DANNY SHOOK THE HARMONICA, put it to his lips again and blew. This time he managed some long notes that he slurred up and down in a forlorn song. It didn't sound like blues, exactly. More like some primitive lament played on a hollow bamboo flute by an ancient cave dweller.

He closed his eyes and let the notes linger in the air.

Then he thought he heard something.

Someone was humming.

He stopped.

The humming went on for a second. Then it stopped.

Danny started playing again. The humming started, too.

Danny stopped. The humming went on.

"Hmmmm..uhhh...ooohh..."

Danny quickly looked around.

"Is someone there?" he said, trying not to sound afraid.

The humming stopped, but still Danny saw nothing.

And then, on the wall across from him, about as high as his shoulders, he saw some dirt fall. Then a little more.

Actually, it didn't just fall. It jumped out, like something was pushing it from behind.

Danny took a step closer. And another. He saw something small push out of the earth.

A small, black snout. The snout was followed by tiny eyes and a sleek head with no visible ears.

A rat?

Danny took a step back.

"Hey, why did you stop playing?" said the animal in a wheezy, grumbly sort of voice. "It was real sweet. Made me think of my mudder."

"What?" Danny said, his eyes wide.

"She used to sing to me. She sang to all us mole pups. That was a long time ago. Is this your hole? Got to say, it's a bit showoffy, don't you think? I mean, you've done a bang-up job and all, but who needs this much room? And by the way, what sort of mole are you? Never seen one so big. Not that I can see very well, of course. And how's the worming around here? Any juicy ones?"

Danny took two more steps forward. He stared at the pinched face of the mole as it sniffed in his direction.

Maybe he was still lying in the dirt. Any minute now he would wake up and this talking Muppet would disappear.

"Hang on a sec," the mole said. It rooted its nose into the dirt wall and pulled out a large black beetle. The beetle waved its legs.

"Want a piece of this?" the mole mumbled, careful not to let go of the beetle.

"No, that's okay."

"More for me-o." It flipped the beetle into the air and caught it again. Snap, gulp. Gone.

This made no sense.

"How come I can understand you?" Danny asked.

"I'm in the dark on that one, as we moles like to say. I guess all moles speak the same language, even if the accent is different. I had a cousin, came from way out past Fat River, used to roll his r's. *R-r-really r-r-raining*, he'd say. And an aunt from Nobby Hill whose voice always went up like she was asking a question. *I love the crunch of armadillo bugs? That mole never washes his whiskers?* Regional variations, you might say. Now, you? You've got a kind of nervous tremble that reminds me of the moles from Mush Valley. You related to them?"

"No. I'm not a mole at all."

"You aren't? Explains the flat face, no offense. What sort of creature are you, then? Come closer. I can't see."

Danny took a step forward.

"Come on. I don't bite. Not often, anyway."

Danny moved closer until his own nose was just inches away from the mole's. The animal had a musky scent.

The mole tilted his head and squinted hard.

"You a pig, maybe?"

"No."

"Porcupine?"

"Uh-uh."

"I give up. Tell me."

"I'm a human."

"A human!"

The mole screamed. It was a terribly loud, high-pitched scream that hurt Danny's ears.

"Why are you screaming?"

"Sorry, sorry. I just…well, not to put too fine a point on it, but humans are … *blah!*"

"Gee, thanks."

"I don't know why you hairless soft-skins can't leave the underground to us. All that digging! All those pipes and wires and hibbledegibbits! Do we smash your houses? Do we rip up your walkways? I mean, I'm not exactly fond of foxes, either, but at least with a fox you know where you stand. But I can see I'm hurting your feelings. My apologies. You can't help what you are. It's just smelly bad luck."

Danny closed his eyes hard. But when he opened them again, the mole was still there.

"If I'm a human and you're a mole, I still don't understand how we can talk to each other," he said.

"How should I know?" said the mole, wagging his head. "You're the one from the so-called higher species. Well, I've got to go a-beetling and a-bugging. Later, human."

"Wait a minute," Danny said.

But the mole had already slipped back into the hole.

5
Most Beautiful Baby

FOR A LONG MOMENT, Danny stared at the hole. He rubbed his forehead and then looked up at the light and blinked.

Real or not, he was a little sorry the mole had gone. The small creature had been interesting, if strange, company.

One thing for sure, he was awake now. And since he was here, he might as well look on the bright side. Being trapped in a hole did have some things going for it. For one thing, nobody was telling him to unload the dishwasher or cut the grass. For another, his brother wasn't grabbing the video game or calling him Danny Dog-breath.

In fact, Danny couldn't remember a time when somebody wasn't bugging him about something.

What's more, his parents were probably starting to ask each other where he was. They were beginning to wonder why he hadn't come home. No doubt they would start looking in the usual places where he liked to hang out — up the tree in the backyard, sprawled on the floor behind his bed. They would stop thinking about themselves for once and start worrying about him.

Hey, Sheila, you don't suppose our son has run away?

No, not Danny. He's too sensible. Doesn't have the imagination.

His revolting brother would be sent out on his bike to check the school yard and the park. They would talk about calling the police.

Do you really think it's necessary, dear? I'm sure the police don't like to be bothered.

Well, let's wait a little longer. He'll probably walk through the door any minute.

They would wait for another hour.

They would become frantic, pacing back and forth, weeping, blaming themselves.

They would call the police.

And when the police officers came to the door, what would his parents say?

Danny was a little upset. Perhaps because we were going to destroy his life by selling the house and making him live in two different places where he has no friends. And, oh yes, we got rid of his dog.

Wouldn't they sound stupid!

Good, Danny thought. Let them worry.

He opened his backpack and dropped in the harmonica. He took out his math textbook, his workbook and his pencil.

He might as well do his homework. In fact,

he wanted to do his homework. It would be a pleasure doing it down here in his hole without anyone bothering him.

Danny opened the book.

A woman has to get to work by nine a.m. It takes her fifteen minutes to take a shower, twenty minutes to have breakfast and thirty minutes to walk to work. What time does she have to get up?

"Ah, this is too easy," he said aloud. He figured out the answer and wrote it down. Then he checked the back of the book.

Wrong.

"Oops." Danny re-did the question. He finished his math homework and then did the bonus questions. He did his grammar homework, too, underlining the adverbs in a series of sentences.

For geography he was supposed to use a dictionary and look up the meanings of the words "village," "town" and "city." Since he didn't have a dictionary, he decided to make up his own definitions.

VILLAGE: A place with a few stores that sell stuff like old-fashioned toffee and straw hats, and the kids swing on a rope over the swimming hole while their dogs jump around and bark, because every kid has a dog.

TOWN: A place with a Main Street, a movie theater and a high-school football team where you used to go to cheer on your brother but now you don't because he's such a jerk.

CITY: Traffic, coffee shops, punk rock clubs, bank tellers with tattoos, schools where kids play the drums all day, and grownups who spend their time trying to fulfill themselves by singing songs in strange languages.

Pretty good, Danny thought. In fact, this was just about the best homework he'd ever done.

What now?

Danny put his books back in the backpack and felt the DVD with his fingers. Too bad he didn't have a DVD player. *School for Zombies 3* was definitely the best of the series. He particularly liked it when the principal of the zombie high school got appointed to a regular school and started to chase the kids around. Then the kids threw basketballs and other stuff at him.

Since he had nothing else to do, he could practice being a zombie.

Danny stood up, stretched out his arms and began walking forward on stiff legs, rocking back and forth, mouth half open.

"Aarrr...ooogghh," he moaned as he stumbled around.

He did a pretty good zombie. But the truth was that down in this dim hole, not knowing how he was going to get out, the thought of zombies was freaking him out a little.

So he stopped being a zombie. And he realized something else.

He needed to pee. Really, really badly.

6

Life Story

ONCE DANNY REALIZED he had to pee, he began to dance on the spot as he looked around. The deep hole in the ground was not, unfortunately, equipped with a toilet.

This, Danny thought, is what they never write about in books.

Fortunately, it was a very big hole. So Danny walked to the other end. Using his shoe, he scraped a hollow out of the soft earth. He aimed carefully. Afterwards he brushed the loose dirt back over it.

Well, that was all right. Just as long as he didn't have to do more than pee.

"So what's your name, anyway?"

Danny spun around. Behind him, looking out of a new hole in the wall, was the mole. His paws were large for his size, like furry oven mitts with long, curved nails. He grunted as he pulled out the rest of his egg-shaped body.

Suddenly, he popped out like a cork and landed flat on the ground.

"Umph!"

"Are you all right?" Danny asked, leaning over.

"Never better." The mole sat up and began to groom his belly.

"I didn't think you were coming back. I didn't think you *could* come back."

The mole stopped to sniff the air.

"Am I wrong, or does it smell like a dog's favorite tree around here?"

"Sorry. We're standing in my washroom. Let's go to the other side. And by the way, my name is Danny."

"Glad to meet you, Darnit."

"Not Darnit. Danny."

"Touchy, you humans. And I'm Mole."

"You don't have a name?"

"That *is* my name. I know. It can be confusing. Somebody calls, 'Hey, Mole!' and everybody in the tunnel turns around. Now, tell me something, Darnit. What exactly are you doing down here?"

"It's a bit of a long story."

"You think I've got something better to do?"

So Danny told the mole what had happened. And although it felt a bit strange to converse with a small, furry animal, Danny was glad to have somebody to listen.

It was a relief to tell it all. The announcement by his parents, how his brother didn't seem to care, his own boiling over, and how he ran and ran until he fell into the hole.

Every so often the mole would ask a question. "So let me get this straight. They're moving to separate holes?" Or, "You mean you actually lived with a dog?" At other times he would make a sympathetic noise — "Ungh!" or "F-f-fah!"

When Danny was finished, the mole said, "That is some story. Good job telling it. Did you make it up yourself?"

"What do you mean, make it up? I didn't make it up at all! That's the whole point. That's what really happened. It's how I got here. It's true."

"Oh, I see," said the mole, rubbing his whiskers. "No wonder you got all hot and bothered. But, frankly, I don't know if living in a hole is the answer. Not that I can tell if you'll be happy as an Undergrounder or not. We moles aren't very good at looking into the future. Truth is, we can't see much past our own noses."

Danny sighed. Maybe there were limits to

talking with a mole. He decided to change the subject.

"So what about you? What's your story?"

"Ah, you're just being polite," said the mole. "You don't want to know."

"I do. I've never heard about a mole's life before."

"Well, then, pull up some earth and open your ears. First — and this is really good — I was born. Naked, blind and deaf. *Waaa! Where's Mudder? I'm scared!* Get it? Then I found her right beside me and began to nurse on her teat. I had to fight my brothers and sisters to get one. They were pushy. And I was the smallest in the litter."

"Where was your father?" asked Danny.

"Who knows? He met Mum, he was like, 'You're the mole of my dreams, babe, let me kiss that cute snout of yours.' And the next minute he's tunneling out of there. So I never met him. But Mudder always said I look like him. Mind you, she said we all look like him."

"That's rough."

"So, anyway, I grew fur, began to hear, opened my eyes. One minute it's cuddling with Mum, sleeping and slurping, the good life. The next minute she's giving us the boot. 'Time to grow up!' she says. 'There's a world of worms out there.' And quick as you can chew through a root, I'm on my own. But I got used to it. And you know, the single life does have its benefits. You can eat in bed, sleep whenever you want. No listening to somebody drone on about the centipede that got away. I was enjoying myself."

"You didn't get lonely?"

"Nah. Moles don't get along with each other. It was just me, myself and I. Had my own tunnel system, a nice nest. Worms and insects would burrow through the earth and drop into my tunnels and I would scoop 'em up. Yup, it was the good life."

The mole sighed. Then he pointed his snout at Danny, and his beady eyes grew hard.

"And then all these big machines came. The ones up top. *Vroom! Gracchh!* They ripped up my home and all my tunnels. I'm digging to save my life! I was so scared I didn't know which way was which. I guess that's how I ended up here. And now I really need to find a new place to scratch my bottom in peace. It was swell chewing the fat. But I'd better go. As we moles say, dandy digging into you."

Danny had hardly taken in all the mole had said before the creature touched his ear — or where his ear might have been — as if tipping an invisible hat. Then he stuck his snout into the earth wall, set his claws on either side, and began digging like a crazed wind-up toy. Earth flew back into Danny's face.

"Hey, wait a minute," Danny called, spitting out dirt.

The mole stopped. Only his rump was visible.

"Yes?" came a muffled voice.

"Do you have to go just yet? The bulldozers won't start up again until Monday. Maybe you could hang around for a while."

The mole's rump wiggled as he reversed his way back out of the hole.

"What's a Monday? Anything like a nice fat grasshopper?"

"Nothing at all. It's hard to explain."

"Oh, drat! Why did I mention grasshoppers? Now I won't be able to stop thinking about them until I have one. Listen, I'll be back. Maybe you can make up another story."

"I didn't make that one up!" Danny said.

But the mole had already turned around again and pulled himself into the hole.

7

The Elements

DANNY STOOD THERE for a while, trying to make sense of everything. Until today, he'd never even seen a *nontalking* mole. Now he knew that they were small, with whiskers and pink noses at the ends of their snouts. Their small eyes were hard to see, and their ears weren't visible at all. Their front paws looked like oven mitts, and their curling claws worked better than shovels. And their fur looked really soft.

They looked like they were made up of pieces left over from regular animals.

Not only did this one talk, but he was a

regular chatterbox, as Danny's mother would say.

She had once actually been a good mother, he remembered, taking care of him when he was sick, making him laugh, bringing him applesauce and toast in bed. But at the moment, Danny liked that mole better than he liked anybody in his family.

He felt something.

A drop of rain. Quickly followed by several more drops. Warm rain, since it was almost summer, but still, Danny didn't want to get wet.

A moment later it became a full shower.

He pushed his backpack against the dirt wall. He sat beside it, knees up, head down. The wall protected him a little, but he was still getting wet, and it wouldn't be long before he was soaked through and sitting in a mud puddle.

What if he caught a cold or got pneumonia?

What if he got a burning fever and started to hallucinate about worse things than talking rodents? What if he started to imagine that zombies were breaking through the walls? Zombies reaching out with their bloody hands, gnashing their rotten teeth and staring with dead eyes as they came toward him?

Danny would never take a roof for granted again.

The rain came down harder. He would have to do something, but what?

He remembered the big garbage bag in his backpack and pulled it out. He could make a poncho by punching in holes for his head and arms, but his head would still get wet and so would the backpack.

Wait a minute.

Danny found the nail clippers. Using the file, he carefully slit the garbage bag along the sides. Unfolded, it was now twice as long. If he attached two corners to the wall and the other two corners to the ground maybe three feet out, he would have a lean-to with a slanted roof that he could crawl under.

But how to attach the corners to the wall?

The paper clips! They were rattling around at the bottom of his backpack.

He fished them out and untwisted the end of one. He hooked it carefully through the plastic bag at the corner. Then he pushed the other end into the wall at an angle so it wouldn't pull out.

He did the same for the other top corner and then for the two corners on the earthen floor.

The rain battered against the plastic, but it held. Danny grabbed his backpack and crawled underneath. He could sit with his knees up quite comfortably and stay dry. A steady trickle of rain poured off the side of the bag.

He had another idea. He took out his thermos and filled it to the top with the rain water coming off the plastic. He took a drink and topped it up again.

Pretty good, Danny thought with a swell of pride. Pretty resourceful, if he did say so himself.

Too bad there was nothing else to do. He thought about pretending to talk to the mole, but that seemed stupid. Clearly he couldn't make the mole appear whenever he wanted, which made him think it might be real. Certainly it didn't feel like a product of his imagination, especially as he didn't have a very good one, according to his parents.

Since he had nothing else to do, he took out his school notebook and pencil. The only homework he still hadn't done was his English assignment. He was supposed to write a story based on his family.

Danny hated English assignments. Why did he have to make up a story? Not everybody was creative. It wasn't fair. He always ended up staring at the blank paper for hours and then finally writing something he knew wasn't any good.

What could he write about his family?

He remembered the DVD in his backpack.

He felt an idea coming on.

He wrote down the title. *The Last One.*

Then he started to write.

Jeff Eldridge knew there was a zombie epidemic. After all, he was twelve years old and extremely smart for his age. He and his family had been watching the news for weeks. Jeff saw lawyers, doctors and teachers marauding through the streets. They walked in their slow, Frankenstein way, one foot and then another, seeking out living humans to feed on.

Jeff knew what happened when you were bitten by a zombie. You turned into one yourself. He also knew that not all zombies had bloodshot eyes and rotting flesh. Some zombies looked normal. They sounded normal, too.

But they weren't. Inside, they were zombies.

When Jeff came home from school and found that his parents had put all their belongings into

cardboard boxes, he naturally thought something weird was going on. But what really turned him onto the truth was when he couldn't find the family dog, Spot.

"Delicious," said his father, wiping his mouth with a bed sheet.

Yes, that's right. Jeff's parents had eaten the family dog!

"I'm still hungry," said Jeff's brother, Donald. And then Donald looked at Jeff. Disgusting drool began to drip from his mouth. His brother and his parents began to move toward him.

And that's when Jeff knew.

His family were all zombies!

Should he run? Or should he try to find a way to turn them back into humans?

Danny was so absorbed in writing his story that it was a while before he realized that the patter sound had stopped.

And that writing sure made a person hungry.

He pulled out a peanut-butter granola bar, tore the wrapper and took a bite. He always liked to carry a few in case he got hungry, and his brother always made fun of him for it. *"Expecting to be caught in a hurricane with nothing to eat?"* he said once.

As Danny chewed, he poked his head from under the plastic and looked up. The sun was coming out again. He crawled out from under the roof, trying to stay out of the muddy spots. He walked around, stretched and shook himself.

He looked up. The circle of light wasn't as bright as before. An unpleasant shiver went through him at the thought of night coming on.

Danny saw a dark shape at the edge of the hole. It was a dog. A dog was looking down at him.

"Worlff!" said the dog.

"Thwack?" he said. "Is that you, boy?"

Thwack whined and scratched at the edge of the hole, knocking in bits of earth.

"Thwack! It is! It is you! You ran away from the farm, just like I ran away, and you found your way back. You missed me, didn't you? You don't want to live without me. Good dog!"

Thwack whimpered and yipped. He darted forward so that Danny was afraid he would fall into the hole, too. But Thwack pulled himself back in time.

He started to run around the hole, yelping and barking.

This was good! Somebody would see the dog acting weird. Somebody would come and find him!

Thwack stopped. Once more he looked down at Danny, one ear half raised and his mouth open as if he was smiling. Then he shook his ears and scratched himself with a hind leg.

A butterfly flitted over his head. He snapped at it.

He trotted off.

"Thwack?"

There was no answer. For several minutes Danny looked up and called, but the dog did not return.

Thwack was a good dog, but Danny had to admit he wasn't the smartest canine in the world. He could be easily distracted. And now he had forgotten Danny.

Suddenly Danny felt intensely lonely. He was still angry at his father and his mother and even his brother, but that didn't mean he wouldn't be overjoyed to hear their voices and see them looking down the hole to find him.

Maybe they hadn't even noticed he was missing. Or maybe they were glad. Selling the house and moving away would be a lot easier without him. That sure would solve all their problems.

It got darker and darker. Danny didn't like the idea of being in the hole when he couldn't see anything.

He crawled under his garbage-bag lean-to. It made him feel a little safer.

He felt cold and took his sweatshirt out of his backpack. He yanked it on, pulling the hood over his head.

His sweatshirt smelled like home. Like his dad's spicy vegetarian stew and his mom's rose incense. He curled up on the ground, the lumpy backpack under his head. For a long time he kept his eyes open in the darkness, listening to faint, distant sounds.

He wished that he had company. Any kind of company.

"Mole?"

But there was no answer. Danny closed his eyes, opened them, then closed them again.

8

O Glorious Dark!

SOMETHING BOPPED DANNY on the head, waking him up.

"Huh?" he muttered.

He opened his eyes. His head and shoulders were sticking out from under the garbage bag. Above him, the sun was shining.

Danny blinked at the circle of bright sky. Then he saw what had bopped him, lying near his nose.

An apple.

Somehow, an apple had fallen into the hole. Maybe the wind had shaken it off a nearby tree, or somebody had thrown it, or it had bounced off a truck.

In any case, he was glad to have it.

Breakfast in bed, Danny thought. He felt the hunger growling in his stomach.

He stood up and stretched. He walked around and ate the apple. It was a Macintosh, crisp and sweet, with only a little bruise where it had hit him. He left nothing but the stem and seeds.

He went to his makeshift washroom to pee. He came back, looked up at the circle of light again and saw a wisp of cloud.

Yesterday he wondered whether his parents were glad he was gone. But in the light of day, he didn't believe it. In fact, his parents must be freaking out about now. His picture was probably on the front page of the newspaper.

He could just imagine the article under the picture, with a big headline.

Hunt for Missing Boy
Distraught Parents Regret Selfishness

A local family is miserable after the disappearance of their wonderful and amazing son, Danny. The boy went missing yesterday after his parents behaved in an unbelievably selfish manner.

"We don't blame him," said Danny's mother between tears. "It's all our fault."

"You couldn't find a greater kid," said his grim-faced father. "We don't even deserve to have a kid like him."

Danny's older brother didn't even try to hide the fact that he had been crying non-stop.

"My brother!" he wailed. "Life isn't worth living without him."

Danny's school friends were also in shock. Several girls said they had broken hearts.

"We hope Danny comes home soon," his father said. "As soon as he does, we're going to buy

him a guitar, an electric scooter and the biggest chemistry set on the market."

The search continues.

Were his parents really that upset? Danny hoped so.

Meanwhile, what he really wanted was some buttery toast and scrambled eggs with plenty of ketchup. Just the thought made his mouth water. And then he would take a nice hot shower and watch TV.

He wanted his regular life back.

Suddenly, he lunged at his backpack. He pulled it open, grabbed a granola bar and stuffed half of it into his mouth, practically choking himself. He shoved in the rest, swallowed, and had a coughing fit.

He took a swig of water.

"Help! Help!" he shouted. "I'm down here! In this hole! Get me out!"

From somewhere above he heard a voice.

"Help! Help! I'm up here! Get me out!"

Danny looked up. About three feet above his head he saw the mole looking out of a hole.

"Are you playing some kind of game?" the mole asked.

"No. And it's not funny."

"Hang on a minute. I'm coming down. Oops!"

The mole squirted out of the hole, somersaulted in the air, bounced off Danny's shoulder and landed flat on his stomach.

"Pha-hoo!" The mole sneezed. "That last step was a doozy. Hey, Darnit, you seem a little down in the dung."

Danny sighed. "I spent the night at the bottom of a hole. I've got nothing to eat but one crummy granola bar. For all I know, my parents have already moved away. At this moment they're slaloming down some mountain or spitting sunflower seeds off the Empire State Building. So how do you think I feel?"

"I think you need to hear a poem."

"What?"

"All moles make up poems. We're famous for 'em. Want to hear?"

Danny didn't like poetry much. Maybe it was because his brother wrote song lyrics and his mother said they were the same as poems and his dad said that Doug was as good as a lot of famous poets. Plus last year Danny's teacher made them learn a poem by heart. "The Lady in the Pea-Green Coat" was forty-two lines long and rhymed "transience" with "puissance," which didn't even sound like a real word. Learning it had been torture.

But he didn't want to offend the mole.

"Sure," he said. "I mean, great. I'd be delighted to hear your poem."

The mole brushed back the fur between where his ears ought to have been. He scurried back a couple of feet for more room and

then stood on his haunches, one paw held in
the air like an actor reciting Shakespeare.

Dark, dark, O glorious dark!
Bathe me in blackness, ooohoo ohooo!

Dirt

   Dirt

      Dirt!

Dig-diggity-diggggg —
      Whirr-whirr-whirr
         Gree-gree-gree

Ah. Ssssweet the cool deep, ding! ding! ding!
      the deep so deep.
Shun the sun, down with day!

Better the smell and touch and inner sight
and the soft, soft, soft mudder earthy
to hug hugg huggggg me.

Ahhhhhhhhh

At the final, whispering sound, the mole lowered his head and remained still.

Danny clapped and whistled. "Wow! That was fantastic."

Mole looked up slowly and smiled. "Ah, you're just buttering me up."

"No, I mean it. That was the best poem I ever heard. Seriously."

"Aw, gee." The mole waddled closer to Danny. "I did feel rather inspired."

Danny looked down at the mole — at his soft fur, his dark snout with its pink tip. He thought of Thwack. His dog loved to be stroked, and petting him always made Danny feel better.

He reached out and said, "Could I pet you?"

"Huh?" The mole jumped a foot into the air and landed on his back. He waved his paws until he managed to right himself.

"I'm sorry," Danny said quickly. "I didn't mean to scare you. Your fur looks soft, that's all."

"It is soft. And, no, you can't pet me. What do I look like? One of those little yappy things you carry around in a purse? I have my dignity, you know. Besides, we have extra-sensitive skin. Helps us find our way in the dark."

"I shouldn't have asked. Sorry."

The mole shook himself all over. "Apology accepted. Moles don't hold grudges. And now you can entertain me."

"Entertain you? How?"

"How do I know? I don't have a clue what you humans can do other than smash things up. But we're having a little artistic gathering here, aren't we? I recited a poem. Now it's your turn."

"Well," Danny said. "I could play my harmonica. But I'm not very good."

"A harmonica? Anything like a rutabaga? I'm not too keen on vegetables."

"It's that thing I was playing when you first came. It makes music."

"Splendid! I love music. Go ahead. I'm all ears. Ear holes, anyway."

So Danny took his harmonica out of the backpack. He drew in a breath, put the instrument to his lips and blew gently. A blurry note emerged. He blew harder and used a series of quick puffs, getting louder and louder. Then he tried some in-and-out breaths, the notes bending back and forth.

Eee-aww...eee-aww!

As the mole listened, he nodded his head back and forth. He began shuffling his back legs, claws tapping the earth. A moment later he was doing what Danny could only call mole-dancing, waving his snout in the air and bouncing his rump up and down.

At last Danny was too out of breath to play anymore. He bleated out one final note. The two panted to catch their breath.

"Yee-hah!" said the mole. "We had ourselves a regular hootenanny! Only thing missing was a jug of moleshine. Made me kind of hungry, though. This time of day, with the sun overhead, it's slim pickings. But there might be some ants still marching. Problem with ants, you eat a few dozen and you're hungry half an hour later. But they're better than nothing. See you later, Darnit."

"You're going again?" Danny asked.

But the mole just turned around and began to dig a new hole, shoveling with amazing speed as his claws tossed dirt into the air.

Another few seconds, and he was gone.

9

Comfort Food

WITHOUT THE MOLE AROUND, time definitely moved more slowly. Danny decided he needed some exercise. Wasn't that what people did in jail? In the movies, prisoners always made sure they stayed in good physical shape.

He paced back and forth fifty times.

He touched his toes.

He did a hundred jumping jacks.

He sat down, exhausted.

Not only exhausted, but hungry.

He only had one granola bar left. Once it was gone, he would have nothing.

Was it possible that he had missed something in his backpack? He hurried over to check every pocket again, feeling in all the little folds and corners.

In the bottom corner of the main compartment he found seven dried-up, lint-covered raisins. They must have fallen out of one of those little snack boxes his mother put in his lunch sometimes.

In a hidden pocket inside a side pocket he found two packets of dairy creamer. He remembered that one day at his dad's office he had gone to fetch a coffee for his father. He had brought back the two packets but his dad didn't want them, so he put them in his backpack.

His dad didn't like his job very much. It had something to do with making sure that shipments of heating oil didn't go to the wrong place by mistake. He'd been doing the same job for, like, fifteen years. His office was pretty drab, and his window looked out onto a tar roof. Worse, his boss was always yelling at him.

Danny had never really thought about how his dad had to spend eight hours a day in that place.

Danny found his thermos and took off the top. Upside down, the top became a small bowl. He ripped open a packet of dairy cream-er and poured the powder into the bowl. He added water and used his pencil to mix them together into something that looked like milk. He broke off half the granola bar and crushed it into the bowl. He picked the lint off four raisins and laid them gently on top.

Cereal!

Without a spoon, Danny had to put the bowl to his lips and use his finger to shovel some of the cereal into his mouth.

Wow, was it good! Especially when he got one of the dry, sweet, chewy raisins along with the soggy granola.

When it was gone he did it all over again, using the second packet of dairy creamer, more water, the last half of the granola bar, and the three remaining raisins.

He remembered an expression he had once heard. Comfort food. Cereal and milk was definitely comfort food.

At home, back in his old life, he always read the cereal box while he ate breakfast. He didn't have a cereal box but he did have the granola-bar wrapper, so he read that.

Used by mountain climbers, desert trekkers and world travelers.

Now they could add *hole dwellers*.

10

Lost Wool and Testy Mouse

EATING THE CEREAL made Danny sleepy. He leaned against the wall beside his garbage-bag shelter and closed his eyes. He dozed on and off as the afternoon waned and the light from above grew softer.

A voice woke him up.

"So, how'd you sleep? Me, like a top. Mind you, moles always sleep well."

"Mole?" Danny said, yawning. He looked up at the dimming light. It was getting late. At home, he would probably be watching TV. His dad might be making popcorn. His mom would ask him how his day went.

He did not want to spend another night in this hole.

"Sure it's me. You think a rat would be down here visiting? Some people mistake us for rats, but we're not anything like 'em," said the mole. "For one thing, rats will eat any old garbage. Disgusting! Moles are much pickier. We insist on organic. All right, rats are clever, but if you ask me that's what gets them into trouble. Scheming all the time. *How can I steal this apple? How can I sneak into that basement?* No wonder people don't like them. People don't have negative feelings about moles. I mean, have you ever called anyone a molefink?"

"No, I guess not."

"Meanwhile, I never met a rat who didn't think it was fun to insult a mole. *Hey, squint eyes! Left your ears in another tunnel? Is that your snout or did you swallow a turnip?* Let me tell you, I've heard them all. But as my mudder taught me just before she booted me out, be a mole and proud of it. And if those rats won't shut up, just put some dirt in your ear holes."

"I'm glad you're here," Danny said.

"Of course I'm here. Here is where I always am. Is it any different for humans?"

"No, I guess not."

"I may not be such a good judge of your species, but you're looking pretty mopey-dopey again."

"It's just that in a few hours it will be night again. I bet new people are already living in our house. What if my parents didn't leave me a note? What if I never even get out of here?"

"Now, now, my young friend," said the mole, tapping Danny's knee with his claws. "Is that any way to talk? Would you like me to cheer you up with some impressions? I'm quite good at them. I can do Angry Mole. Or

Mole in Love. Or Mole Smacking His Snout into a Rock, or — "

"I don't think so. I'm just not in the mood," Danny said. "But maybe you could help me with something."

"Name it."

"Help me write my Last Will and Testament."

"Sure. But what is a Lost Wool and Testy Mouse? Sounds to me like a mouse dressed up as a sheep. No wonder he's in a bad mood."

Danny looked in his backpack for a pencil and a workbook.

"It's what a human writes before he dies. It says where he wants all his stuff to go. Who should own it."

"Very interesting. Maybe we moles should have a Lost Wool and Testy Mouse, too. Except we don't have any stuff."

Danny started to write in the workbook,

and as he wrote he spoke the words out loud.

"The last will...and testament of...Daniel Ronald Diamond."

"Who's that?"

"That's my full name. Do you know how to spell bequeath?"

"I don't even know how to spell 'spell'."

"I don't suppose spelling matters." He began to write again.

"I, Daniel Ronald Diamond, being of sound mind and body, but possibly going to die from falling in a hole, bequeath the following possessions. My collection of model cars goes to..."

Danny hesitated.

"Who?" asked the mole.

"To my father. Because he and I always played with them when I was little."

"Nice," said the mole. "What's next?"

"The sunset painting on the fridge goes to my mother. Because she said that it made her feel happy and sad at the same time."

"Good."

"My bike, my music player and my comic books go to my brother, because he taught me how to ride and how to make a stink bomb."

"Valuable skills, I'm sure," the mole said.

Danny closed the workbook. "I guess that's it. They can figure out what to do with my clothes and other junk."

Danny felt like crying.

"If you don't mind me asking," said the mole. "What about your harmonica? I mean, that's a pretty nice item. Any person — even any *animal* — would be glad to have it."

Danny looked at the mole. The little creature gazed at him with his head tilted to one side and his pink mouth open. He looked just like Thwack when he wanted to play Fetch. It made Danny want to laugh.

He opened the workbook again.

"My harmonica goes to the mole who kept me good company during my final hours."

The mole covered his face. "Aw, I'm blushing. On the inside, I mean."

"Now I'll just sign it," Danny said. "And you also have to sign it as the witness."

Danny held out the pencil.

"Do I chew it or put it up my nose?"

"Neither. Hold it like this. That's good. Now just make an X on the paper."

"An X?"

"Think of it as one tunnel crossing another."

"Got it." The mole held the pencil between his paws with the end in his mouth. He managed to make one squiggly line and then cross it with another.

"Perfect," Danny said. He took the pencil and notebook and put them in his backpack.

It was a solemn moment. They remained quiet for some time after. The light dimmed a little more.

Then Danny saw something that made him stare.

His backpack was moving.

It seemed to rise up an inch or so and then slide sideways before becoming still again.

Had he imagined it? Quite a few unbelievable things had happened lately.

The backpack moved again.

"Uh, Mole…"

"Yes, Darnit?"

"I think my backpack just — "

And at that moment the thing *under* the backpack, the thing that had caused it to move, darted out so quickly that Danny froze in surprise.

And then the mole was a whirling blur of dirt and fur.

"Aaee!" screamed the mole.

"What is it, what is it?" cried Danny, staring without understanding. And then the whirling stopped and Danny saw.

It was a snake. A snake was coiled tightly around the mole.

"I...can't...breathe..."

"You won't need to in a minute," hissed the snake. Its narrow head undulated back and forth over the mole. "Here I thought it was bad luck to have fallen into this hole last night. And look what I find! A nice fat mole for dinner. Why, I won't need to eat for a week."

"Get...off!" Mole sputtered, trying to push his claws against the snake.

"Very good." The snake nodded its head. "Every time you breathe out, I tighten a little more. It won't be long now."

Danny felt such horror that he still hadn't moved. But now he took a step toward the snake in spite of his terror.

"Let go of him! Stop hurting my friend."

"Come any closer and I'll bite you!" trilled the snake. "And won't I enjoy that!"

Danny stepped back again.

Mole gasped. "Don't...get...near..."

But he couldn't say more.

What to do? What to do? Mole was having the life squeezed out of him right in front of Danny. The little creature's eyes were bulging. A spot of foam had gathered at the side of his mouth. His paws stopped twitching.

This was terrible!

Danny looked wildly around. He saw his backpack and grabbed it. He dumped everything out. Nothing seemed of use until he saw the end of his metal ruler. He pulled it out, held one end, and almost without thinking turned around and smacked the snake on the head with the other end.

Wang!

"Oooh," moaned the snake, shaking its head. "That hurt. You'd better not try it again or — "

Wang!

"Arrr! I said stop that." The snake's head wobbled up and down. Danny could see it

loosen its coils just a little. Mole managed to suck in a breath before the snake tightened its grip again.

"You want to play tough, do you?" The snake opened its jaws and showed its small but sharp white fangs. "I can strike pretty far, you know. And I can just about reach your —"

Wang!

"Ahh! Don't you dare —"

Wang! Wang! Wang!

The snake's head sank to the ground and its coils slackened enough for Mole to scramble his way out. The exhausted little creature, panting for air, crawled behind Danny and half buried himself in the ground.

"Wang it again!" the mole cried.

But Danny held back. He grasped the ruler at one end as if it were a sword, ready to swing if necessary.

The snake was slowly moving, trying to regain its balance. It shakily raised its head, looking at Danny.

"Now you get out of here," Danny said. "I don't know how, exactly, but you'd better. Or I really will smack you. I'm just giving you one last chance."

"All right, all right," said the snake, coiling itself up. "There's no need for more violence. After all, everyone needs to eat. It's the chain of life. I'm just a link in the chain like everything else. No better or worse."

"Maybe," said Danny. "But today there's no mole on the menu."

"Yes, yes. I know when I've lost. Let me just clear my head and then I'll find a hole or some other way to crawl out of here."

"Darnit," said the mole.

"What?"

"You know my eyesight isn't too good. Is the snake all coiled up?"

"Yup."

"Because that's what a snake does just before it —"

The snake made a sudden lunge for Danny, its jaws wide. But Danny had not taken his eyes off it. Like a baseball player at bat, he was ready.

Wang!

"Owww!"

The snake cried out but it did not give up. Quickly it coiled itself for another strike.

Danny stepped forward. He grasped the

ruler at the end with both hands and shoved it under the snake. Then he pulled his arms up with all his might.

"Wha....?"

Danny flung the snake into the air.

High, high, higher it went, hissing and cursing all the way.

"What's happening, what's happening?" the mole asked.

Danny looked up. In the air above the hole, a large bird was circling.

A hawk had spotted the commotion below. Now Danny saw it dive down at great speed and dip into the hole just as the snake rose from below.

The hawk grasped hold of the snake with its talons. Flapping its wide wings, it pulled itself out of the hole and rose into the air again. A moment later it was out of sight.

"Darnit?" said the mole. "Tell me what happened."

Danny looked up at the empty circle of sky. "The chain of life," he said quietly. "That's what happened."

11

Big Questions

DANNY AND THE MOLE were so rattled by the snake attack that it took them a long time to calm down. The mole groomed his ruffled fur and chattered away.

"Snakes, I hate 'em," he said. "They're worse than rats. You can talk reason to a rat, if you ignore the sarcasm. Sometimes a rat will even give you a heads-up about a cat prowling nearby. But snakes? They're cold-blooded, they are. Not an ounce of compassion..."

Danny took a long swig of water, finishing the last drop in the thermos. He put back all the things that he had dumped out of his backpack. He sat down on the ground and leaned against the dirt wall.

He felt as if most of the anger had leaked out of him.

The sky was getting dark.

"Darnit?"

"I know what you're going to say," Danny sighed.

"You do?"

"You're going to say that I should forgive my parents for messing everything up. That I shouldn't give up on them."

"That's not exactly — "

"You're going to say that somebody's got to be the sensible one in the family. That they need somebody around who doesn't just make crazy decisions."

"Like deciding to fall in a hole, you mean?" asked Mole.

"That was an accident."

"Oh."

"I guess when something scary happens it makes you think about your life. I mean, I just watched you almost get eaten by a snake."

"You're telling me."

"Compared to that, living in New York City and Banff for a while doesn't seem so bad. I mean, there are a million things to do in New York, right?"

"At least a million," Mole said.

"And in Banff you can hike and ski and snowboard. There are mountains covered in snow. And cool animals like bears and wolves."

"Wolves?"

"It isn't forever. Maybe we can all have holidays together. Don't get me wrong. I don't approve of their behavior one bit. But they are my parents. It's not like I can avoid them completely. And without me they're going to mess things up even worse. Do you think that's right, Mole? Mole?"

Danny looked over at the mole. The animal had fallen asleep on his back, with his feet in the air. Danny watched his little round stomach rise and fall.

Mole had such a simple life. Digging holes, eating worms, making up poems. Humans were too complicated.

A sound made Danny look up.

"Worllff."

"Thwack?"

Sure enough, it was. Danny could see his outline against the darkening sky. The dog began to whimper and scratch at the edge of the hole.

"Good dog, Thwack! You came back. Look, Mole, it's Thwack!"

"Huh, what?" Mole said, stirring.

"My dog."

"Dog!" Once more the mole scurried behind Danny. "I hate dogs the most. After snakes, anyway."

"Thwack wouldn't hurt a fly. He wants to go home, too. I want to get out of this hole. I want to go back to my family."

At that moment he saw a flashing light at the edge of the hole. Then he saw the silhouette of a figure — a human figure.

"Hey, Henry, you sure this dog isn't crazy? I don't see anything. Wait a minute. Hello? This is the fire department. Is anyone down there?"

Danny began to wave his arms and jump up and down.

"Yes, somebody's down here! I am! Danny Diamond! I'm down here!"

The flash of light became a beam. Danny blinked as it formed a yellow circle around him.

"Well, I'll be," said the firefighter. "It's the missing kid. Are you all right?"

"Yes."

"Be careful, there's a rat right beside you."

The mole snorted. "I've never been so insulted in all my life."

"We've been looking all over for you," the firefighter said. "Tell you what, Danny. We're going to lower a ladder and then I'm going to climb down. And then we'll climb back up together, all right?"

"Okay."

Danny saw more figures surrounding the hole and a lot of people talking at once. Then a very long ladder was lowered.

Danny saw a rather alarmed expression on the mole's face.

"I don't like the looks of that," the mole said.

"That's just so I can climb out."

The end of the ladder came down. Danny grabbed hold of it and guided it to the ground.

"That's it!" he shouted up.

"Hold on, I'm coming," the firefighter shouted back. Danny saw him get on the ladder and start moving down, one rung at a time.

Danny crouched down beside the mole.

"You've been really great," he said. "I don't think I could have made it without you."

"Ah, don't mention it."

"I don't suppose you want to come and live with me."

"Yeesh, what an idea! You want to keep me in a cage with an exercise wheel, maybe?

Take me to school in a shoebox for show-and-tell?"

"I didn't think of it that way."

"Besides, I have to be going. I have some questions of my own, you know. Is there really a Great Mole in the sky? Do worms have feelings? Get it? That's what life is. Questions."

"I guess you're right."

"I know I'm right. Besides, there's this certain, uh, female mole who lives just underneath the park."

"Oh, really," said Danny, smiling. "Do you *like* her?"

"I never said that!" The mole stamped a back paw. "But she does have an awfully cute snout. And those beady eyes! To die for. Listen, if you really want to, go ahead and pet me. A quick stroke or two couldn't hurt."

"You mean it?"

"Just don't make a big thing of it."

Danny reached out and ran his hand over Mole's back. His fur was like velvet, softer than anything he'd ever felt in his life.

"Wow."

"I really hope things work out for you, Darnit. May all your tunnels be dry."

The mole nodded his head and turned around. A second later he was throwing up earth with his claws. Then Danny could only see his rump and little tail.

And then he was gone.

"Hey, wait a minute," called Danny.

From his backpack he pulled out the harmonica. He pushed it halfway into the hole.

There was a pause before the rest of the harmonica disappeared.

"Btheeehh!"

"Bye, Mole," Danny whispered.

12
Pizza

"WHAT WAS THAT FUNNY noise?" said the firefighter as he reached the ground.

"I sneezed," Danny said. "Must be the damp. I hope I'm not catching a cold."

The firefighter put a hand on Danny's shoulder.

"We're just glad to find you. Your parents are pretty upset."

"They are?"

"Of course. Ready to return to the surface?"

"Yes, sir."

Danny started to climb the ladder, the firefighter just behind him. He couldn't wait to get to the top.

When he reached the edge of the hole, there was a burst of applause, but it was hard for him to see because of the bright lights pointed at him.

And then he was standing in the world again. That's what it felt like. Danny had never breathed such wonderful, fresh air. Even in the late evening light everything looked brilliant to him — the leaves on the trees across the road, the wispy clouds in the sky.

It was all simply amazing.

Fire trucks were lined up along the side of the road, their red lights turning. One by one the firefighters shook Danny's hand. A woman came out of the back of an ambulance. She was carrying a medical kit. She looked into Danny's eyes with a light and took his pulse. She asked him weird questions like what school did he go to and what was his brother's middle name. She took a juice box from her kit and pulled off the straw.

"Drink this," she said. "Actually, you're in pretty good shape." Everyone smiled. Danny sucked up the drink.

The first firefighter said, "We'll drive you over to your parents. We just have to put our gear away."

"Okay."

The firefighters began to put the ladders

and ropes and axes back onto the trucks. The two ambulance attendants packed up the medical equipment.

While they were busy, Danny began to walk slowly away. His legs felt wobbly at first, but he kept going, glancing back to make sure nobody had noticed.

He got to the fence and let himself out.

"Hey, Thwack!"

There was his dog, his very own dog, running up and wagging his tail madly, which made his whole backside wiggle.

Danny leaned down and hugged Thwack, who licked his face all over.

"You're such a good dog," Danny said happily. "You didn't forget about me. Come on."

They began to walk. Danny passed the low apartment buildings, then the plaza of small shops — discount eyewear, bagel bakery, shoe repair. All closed. He crossed the park, the swings empty and the teeter-totter tipped to one side. Thwack trotted beside him as he looked into the windows of the Blue Skies Credit Union and Frida's Clothing Exchange. Somebody was mopping the floor of the Strong Brew Coffee Shop.

He went from Nordheim Boulevard to Winkler Avenue to Essex Street.

When he reached his own street, he slowed down. Three police cars lined the curb. But the street itself was deserted. There wasn't a single person around.

Danny stopped for a moment and looked down at Thwack.

"I know this is a weird question," he said. "But do you talk, by any chance? You're not holding out on me, are you?"

Thwack looked at him, head tilted.

"Okay." Danny patted the dog between the ears. "I just wanted to be sure."

When he tried his front door, it opened.

He stepped inside with Thwack behind him.

The house was silent. The magazines on the coffee table sat in neat piles. The dishes were washed and lined up in the rack by the kitchen sink.

The packing boxes were gone. The books and pictures and lamps were back in their places.

Danny went up the stairs and looked into his parents' room. The bed was made and everything was tidy.

Then he saw his sunset painting. Someone had taken it off the fridge and propped it up on his mother's bedside table.

He went into his own room. Everything was just as he had left it. The plastic airplane models hanging from the ceiling. His *Putnick's Guide to the Animal Kingdom* and his science-fiction novels.

He looked out the window.

Police officers were walking up the sidewalk. And with them were Danny's mother and his father and his brother.

Their heads hung down. Some of the policemen at the back carried pizza boxes.

Danny watched as they trooped into the house and went into the kitchen. He could hear their footsteps, their soft voices.

Thwack whimpered.

"Come on, boy," Danny whispered. He walked to the top of the stairs. His heart beat fast. He came down the carpeted steps one at a time, reached the bottom and walked to the kitchen.

He stood at the doorway and looked in. His mother and father sat at the table. His mother's eyes were red. His father needed a shave.

His brother was standing at the window over the sink looking into the backyard at their old swing set.

The pizza boxes were on the table, but nobody had opened them. Police officers stood around looking in their notebooks or speaking quietly to one another.

Thwack smelled the pizza. He bounded past Danny and skidded up to the table, tail thumping.

"Thwack?" Danny's father said, looking surprised. He began to ruffle the dog's ears. "How did you get here, boy? You ran all the way from the farm? Oh, is it great to see you. I'm sorry, boy. I'm so sorry."

Danny's mother looked up. When she saw him her hand went up to her mouth.

"Danny!"

Everyone looked at him.

There was a lot that Danny wanted to say to his mother and father and brother. But he couldn't just yet.

So he said, "Can I have a piece of pizza? I'm really hungry."

And then the three of them rushed over and everyone was hugging him. His brother broke away to get him a piece of pizza. He gave it to Danny, who held it with both hands and took a big bite.

"It's hot," he said.

"Oh, Danny," his mother said as she began to cry. "You're home."

Danny took another bite. And then he thought of another thing to say.

"Is it hard to learn to ski?"

CARY FAGAN is an award-winning author of books for children and adults. He has been nominated for the Toronto Book Award four times, and he has won the Jewish Book Award and the World Storytelling Award. He has been a finalist for the TD Canadian Children's Literature Award, the Mr. Christie's Book Award, the Norma Fleck Award, the Rocky Mountain Book Award, the Manitoba Young Readers' Choice Award and the Blue Spruce Award. His most recent children's novel, *Banjo of Destiny*, was a finalist for the Silver Birch Express Award.

Cary lives with his family in Toronto. www.caryfagan.com

MILAN PAVLOVIC is an illustrator and graphic artist whose drawings, illustrations, paintings and comics have been published and exhibited internationally. He teaches at OCAD University and lives with his family in Toronto. milanpavlovic.net